SALCOTT, THE INDIAN BOY

Story by Melinda Eldridge

Illustrations by Shirley V. Beckes

Raintree Publishers
Milwaukee

Dedicated to my family and J.B.
Little Elementary.   —M.E.

For two special girls, Jennifer and
Anna-Leena.   —S.B.

Copyright © 1990 Raintree Publishers Limited Partnership

1 2 3 4 5 6 7 8 9   93 92 91 90 89

Library of Congress Number: 89-10339

Library of Congress Cataloging-in-Publication Data

Eldridge, Melinda
  Salcott, the Indian boy.

  Summary: Salcott must prove his maturity and bravery by spearing Bear of No Water through the heart.
  1. Indians of North America—Juvenile fiction.   2. Children's writings, American.   [1. Indians of North America—Fiction.   2. Courage—Fiction.   3. Children's writings.] I. Title.
PZ7.E383Sal   1989 [Fic]—dc20   89-10339
ISBN 0-8172-2778-4

Salcott the Indian boy lived in the village of Mothstroat with his mother, father, and little sister. His father Tuthscot was a great warrior, his mother Mayone was the finest weaver in Mothstroat, and his sister Enoz was just his sister.

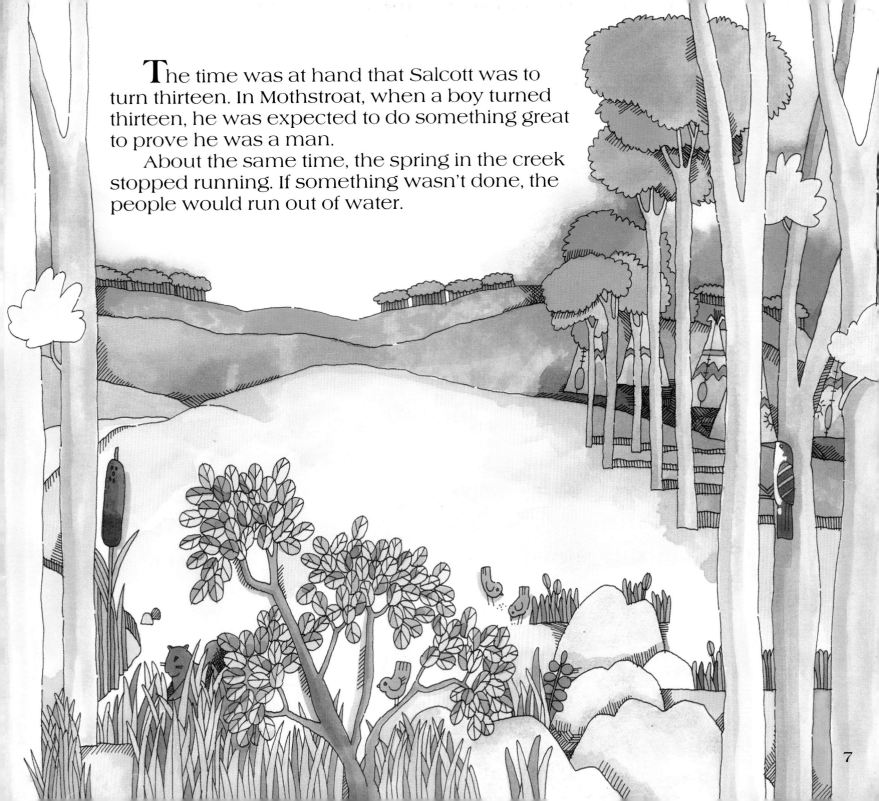

The time was at hand that Salcott was to turn thirteen. In Mothstroat, when a boy turned thirteen, he was expected to do something great to prove he was a man.

About the same time, the spring in the creek stopped running. If something wasn't done, the people would run out of water.

One night, the council called Salcott to attend their meeting. The chief said, "Salcott, we have decided on your task. You are to spear the heart of the Bear of No Water that lives in the cave at the foot of Great Mountain. When blood rushes from the bear's heart, water will rush from the spring. But if you miss the center of its heart, the spring will stop forever."

The next day, Salcott set out on his quest with a basket of food, a blanket, and a spear. He traveled through many dark forests and climbed many hills before he at last reached Great Mountain. The Bear of No Water's cave was on the opposite side, so that meant another day's hike. Finally, Salcott reached the cave. That night he slept lightly, afraid of what might happen the next day.

In the morning, Salcott ate breakfast, then picked up his spear and torch, and marched into the mouth of the cave. Inside, the cave was huge. By the light of his torch, he could see it went far back into the mountain.

Suddenly, Salcott heard a growl from deep within the cave. Grasping his spear, he walked into a tunnel from which the noise seemed to be coming. Along the way, he noticed many strange formations. On the walls, he saw what looked like ancient drawings.

15

The tunnel ended in a large room with many passageways leading out of it. Salcott didn't know which one to choose because the growl seemed to come from all sides. Finally, he chose the corridor from which the noise seemed the loudest. Quietly, he entered.

The tunnel wasn't very long, and soon Salcott found himself right around the corner from the ferocious beast. Then he remembered the chief's warning about missing the center of the bear's heart. Salcott took a deep breath and walked around the corner. There he saw a gigantic bear sleeping on its side.

19

Salcott tiptoed across the room holding his spear and took aim. At the last moment, he looked into the bear's face. It was so peaceful and content looking that Salcott didn't know what to do. Suddenly, he was filled with sadness. He could not bring himself to throw the spear.

Salcott's hand grew weak, and the spear dropped to the floor with a clang. The bear awoke and turned to face him. It looked at the spear on the floor and then at Salcott. It didn't seem alarmed or angry. Instead it sat up and stared at him.

Tears ran down Salcott's cheeks, but they were not tears of fear, they were tears of defeat. The bear seemed to understand and, with compassion in its heart, handed Salcott his spear. Salcott took the spear and slowly walked out of the cave.

Salcott was confused. All the way home, he thought about the bear. He was also worried about what would happen when he got back to the village.

After many days, he reached Mothstroat. There he found much merry-making. Slowly, he dragged his feet into the chief's tent, where all the men of the village had gathered to await his return.

When he walked in, he was received with great honors. Salcott did not understand why they were treating him this way, so he asked the chief.

The chief said, "A spirit came and told me all about what happened. Even though the Bear of No Water's heart did not pour with blood, it poured with compassion, and water has come back to the spring." Salcott then understood and was happy and content.

31

April 28, 1989, was proclaimed "Melinda Eldridge Day" in Arlington, Texas, in honor of Melinda's grand-prize-winning story, *Salcott, the Indian Boy*. The only fifth grader of four grand-prize winners, Melinda also had the honor of being the only winner chosen unanimously by Raintree Publishers' panel of judges. But winning is something that comes naturally to Melinda. She has won many awards in recent years, especially for her writing.

Writing, however, is only one part of Melinda's life. Outside of spending time with her family, which includes her parents and a younger brother, Melinda has many hobbies. She enjoys reading, playing chess, sewing, and collecting dolls. Salcott's story, in fact, came out of one of the family's pastimes—storytelling.

Melinda first came up with Salcott while on a family trip to Missouri in 1988. When she was given the assignment of writing for the Raintree contest, she put Salcott's story on paper—but not before rewriting it many times. As the tale reached its final form, Melinda was especially concerned about whether Salcott should succeed in killing the bear. Her answer to that question, of course, became the whole point of the story.

The twenty honorable-mention winners in the **1989 Raintree Publish-A-Book Contest** were: Andy Binder, Rochester Hills, Michigan; Lauren Boyle, Melrose Park, Pennsylvania; Michael B. Cain, Annapolis, Maryland; Kristin Dehring, Bridgman, Michigan; Caitlin E. Foito, Bellevue, Washington; Emily Gilbert, Dayton, Ohio; Cameron Gordon, Harrisburg, Illinois; Jessica Gordon, Hidden Hills, California; JC Gossett, Roseland, New Jersey; Meghan Gurgol, Troy, Michigan; Andy Hoopes, Afton, Wyoming; Kelli Hutchinson, Faulkton, South Dakota; Amanda Michelle Lee, Lyons, Wisconsin; Christopher C. Martin, Woodward, Oklahoma; Anna Messick, Harrisburg, Pennsylvania; Nicholas Mey, Brighton, Michigan; Stephanie Potter, Plano, Texas; Jennifer Prestwood, Mary Esther, Florida; Joe Steed, Monmouth, Oregon; Nicholas Vogt, Lakeview, Arizona.

Artist Shirley V. Beckes has been illustrating children's books for sixteen years. She graduated from Columbus College of Art and Design. Shirley, her husband, David, and her daughter, Jennifer, live in the Milwaukee area, where she and David have their studio, Beckes Design/Illustration.